mirror ✦ mirror

A Book of Reversible Verse

Marilyn Singer • *illustrated by* **Josée Masse**

Dutton Children's Books   An imprint of Penguin Group (USA) Inc.

Thanks to Steve Aronson, Amy Livingston, Mark McVeigh,
and to all the good folks at Dutton.

DUTTON CHILDREN'S BOOKS
A division of Penguin Young Readers Group

Published by the Penguin Group

Penguin Group (USA) Inc., 375 Hudson Street, New York, New York 10014, U.S.A.

Penguin Group (Canada), 90 Eglinton Avenue East, Suite 700, Toronto, Ontario, M4P 2Y3 Canada

(a division of Pearson Penguin Canada Inc.) • Penguin Books Ltd, 80 Strand, London WC2R 0RL, England

Penguin Ireland, 25 St Stephen's Green, Dublin 2, Ireland (a division of Penguin Books Ltd) • Penguin Group (Australia),

250 Camberwell Road, Camberwell, Victoria 3124, Australia (a division of Pearson Australia Group Pty Ltd)

Penguin Books India Pvt Ltd, 11 Community Centre, Panchsheel Park, New Delhi - 110 017, India • Penguin Group (NZ),

67 Apollo Drive, Rosedale, North Shore 0632, New Zealand (a division of Pearson New Zealand Ltd) • Penguin Books

(South Africa) (Pty) Ltd, 24 Sturdee Avenue, Rosebank, Johannesburg 2196, South Africa

Penguin Books Ltd, Registered Offices: 80 Strand, London WC2R 0RL, England

Text copyright © 2010 by Marilyn Singer

Illustrations copyright © 2010 by Josée Masse

All rights reserved.

CIP DATA AVAILABLE

Published in the United States by Dutton Children's Books,

a division of Penguin Young Readers Group

345 Hudson Street, New York, New York 10014

www.penguin.com/youngreaders

Designed by Sara Reynolds and Abby Kuperstock

Made in U.S.A. • First Edition

ISBN 978-0-525-47901-7

3   5   7   9   10   8   6   4   2

To poets and pals

Rebecca Kai Dotlich
Betsy Franco
Kris O'Connell George
Jane Yolen

m. s.

To Luc, with gratitude

for all his help and support

j.m.

In Reverse

Who
says
it's true—
down
is
the only view?
If you believe that,
this poem
will challenge
you.
Up
is
something new.

Something new
is
up.
You
will challenge
this poem
if you believe that
the only view
is
down.
It's true.
Says
who?

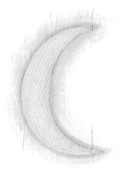

Cinderella's Double Life

Isn't life unfair?
Stuck in a corner,
while they're waiting for a chance
with the prince,
dancing waltz after waltz
at the ball,
I'll be shining
these shoes
till the clock strikes midnight.

Till the clock strikes midnight,
these shoes!
I'll be shining
at the ball,
dancing waltz after waltz
with the prince
while they're waiting for a chance,
stuck in a corner.
Isn't life unfair?

The Sleeping Beauty and the Wide-Awake Prince

Typical.
Hacking through briars,
looking for love—
the prince at work.
But I have to be
sleeping,
never
partying,
never
out in the world.
It's no fun being
in a fairy tale.

In a fairy tale
it's no fun being
out in the world,
never
partying,
never
sleeping.
But I have to be
the prince at work,
looking for love,
hacking through briars.
Typical.

Rapunzel's Locks

No wonder she felt snippy.
Sweeping the floor
it took forever to manage—
all that pale, tangled, dangling hair.
Cut off,
shut up in the tower,
who was
that strange girl with the weird name?
You know,
someone said her mother was a witch.
It figures.

It figures.
Someone said her mother was a witch.
You know
that strange girl with the weird name,
who was
shut up in the tower,
cut off
all that pale, tangled, dangling hair?
It took forever to manage
sweeping the floor.
No wonder she felt snippy.

In the Hood

In my hood,
skipping through the wood,
carrying a basket,
picking berries to eat—
juicy and sweet
what a treat!
But a girl
mustn't dawdle.
After all, Grandma's waiting.

After all, Grandma's waiting,
mustn't dawdle . . .
But a girl!
What a treat—
juicy and sweet,
picking berries to eat,
carrying a basket,
skipping through the wood
in my 'hood.

The Doubtful Duckling

Someday
I'll turn into a swan.
No way
I'll stay
an ugly duckling,
stubby and gray.
Plain to see—
look at me.
A beauty I'll be.

A beauty I'll be?
Look at me—
plain to see,
stubby and gray.
An ugly duckling
I'll stay.
No way
I'll turn into a swan
someday.

Mirror Mirror

Let me help you get some rest.
Mother knows best.
Listen to *me*,
Snow White.
Sleepy, Dopey, Happy,
you've been working day and night.
You look worn out.
A long nap?
A blanket?
An apple to eat?
What would you like?
Time to get off your feet.

Time to get off your feet.
What would you like?
An apple to eat?
A blanket?
A long nap?
You look worn out.
You've been working day and night
Sleepy, dopey, happy
Snow White,
listen to me.
Mother knows best.
Let me help you get some rest.

Full of Beans

What will happen next?
Little does he know.
A giant
beanstalk is about to reach
the
clouds
through the
fragrant green air.
A boy waits in the
garden,
cow, market, beans
leading to this moment:
Time to climb.

Time to climb.
Leading to this moment:
cow, market, beans,
garden.
A boy waits in the
fragrant green air.
Through the
clouds
the
beanstalk is about to reach
a giant.
Little does he know
what will happen next.

Bears in the News

ASLEEP IN CUB'S BED,
BLONDE
STARTLED BY
BEARS,
the headline read.
Next day
Goldilocks claimed,
"They shouldn't have left
the door
unlocked."
She
ate the porridge.
She
broke
a chair.
"Big deal?
No!
They weren't there."

They weren't there.
No
big *deal*?!
A chair
broke.
She
ate the porridge.
She
unlocked
the door.
"They shouldn't have left,"
Goldilocks claimed.
Next day
the headline read:
BEARS STARTLED
BY BLONDE
ASLEEP IN CUB'S BED.

Have Another Chocolate

Fatten up, boy!
Don't you
like prime rib?
Then your hostess, she will roast you
goose.
Have another chocolate.
Eat another piece of gingerbread.
When you hold it out,
your finger
feels like
a bone.
Fatten up.
Don't
keep her waiting . . .

Keep her waiting.
Don't
fatten up.
A bone
feels like
your finger
when you hold it out.
Eat another piece of gingerbread,
have another chocolate—
Goose!
Then your hostess, she will roast you
like prime rib.
Don't you
fatten up, boy!

Do You Know My Name?

Do you know my name?
Think of straw turned to gold.
In this story.
I am
famous
but not
liked.
I am
betrayed
by greed,
a girl,
my foolish self.

My foolish self—
a girl
by greed
betrayed.
I am liked,
but not
famous.
I am
in this story.
Think of straw turned to gold.
Do you know my name?

Disappointment

The princess
who kissed
that frog.
He stayed green.
He kept croaking.
"Shame on you!
Once only,
you
fool!"
she cried
when he tried for a second kiss.
She couldn't believe
such disappointment.
Isn't
this
a fairy tale?
Where's the happy ending?

Where's the happy ending?
A fairy tale
this
isn't.
Such disappointment!
She couldn't believe
when he tried for a second kiss.
She cried.
"Fool
you
once only—
shame on you!"
he kept croaking.
He stayed green,
that frog
who kissed
the princess.

Longing for Beauty

A beast
can love
beauty.
A moist muzzle
can welcome
a rose.
A hairy ear
can prize
a nightingale, singing.
Beneath fur,
look!
A soft heart
stirs,
longing.

Longing
stirs
a soft heart.
Look
beneath fur.
A nightingale singing,
can prize
a hairy ear.
A rose
can welcome
a moist muzzle.
Beauty
can love
a Beast.

The Road

It may be such
a fairy-tale secret,
this much
I know:
The road leads
wherever
you need to go.

You need to go
wherever
the road leads—
I know
this much.
A fairy-tale secret?
It may be such.

ABOUT THE REVERSO

We read most poems down a page. But what if we read them up? That's the
question I asked myself when I created the *reverso*. When you read a reverso
down, it is one poem. When you read it up, with changes allowed only in
punctuation and capitalization it is a different poem.

The first reverso I wrote was inspired by my cat, August:

A cat
without
a chair:
Incomplete.

Incomplete:
A chair
without
a cat.

I had such a good time composing it that I had to write more.

Reversos can be about many topics. However, the reversos in this book
are based on fairy tales. The form is especially appropriate for telling two
sides of one story. It is a form that is both challenging and fun—rather like
creating and solving a puzzle.

Try it yourself and you'll see what I mean!